How the Turtle Got Its Shell

TALES FROM AROUND THE WORLD

By Justine and Ron Fontes

Illustrated by Keiko Motoyama

🌷 A GOLDEN BOOK • NEW YORK

Golden Books Publishing Company, Inc., New York, New York 10106

© 2001 Golden Books Publishing Company, Inc. All rights reserved. Printed in the U.S.A. No part of this book may be reproduced or copied in any form without written permission from the copyright owner. GOLDEN BOOKS®, A GOLDEN BOOK®, A LITTLE GOLDEN BOOK®, G DESIGN®, and the distinctive spine are registered trademarks of Golden Books Publishing Company, Inc. Library of Congress Catalog Card Number: 00-102793   ISBN:0-307-96007-2 A MMI   First Edition 2001

Hello! I am Professor Terry Pin. Today I shall attempt to answer a question as tough as a turtle's shell: How *did* the turtle get its shell?

Turtles appear in legends all around the world. In fact, some people used to believe the world rested on the back of a giant turtle!

One story from China says the universe is a turtle—and the starry sky is on the inside of its enormous shell!

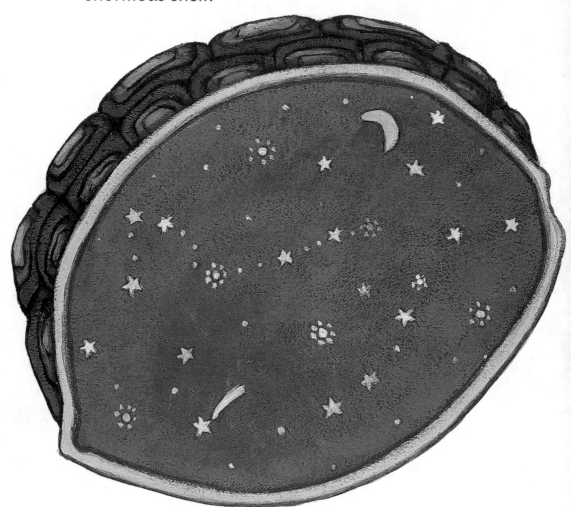

But now it is time to hear some stories that explain how the shell came to be.

Our first tale is from the Algonquian Native Americans.

A long time ago, a handsome, clever god named
Glooskap visited his uncle. Uncle was very kind
but lonely. He couldn't find anyone to marry him.

Glooskap decided to help him. He said, "Wear my clothes to the dance tonight and you will be as handsome as I am."

Uncle did as Glooskap suggested and, sure enough, the chief's most beautiful daughter fell instantly in love with him. This made all the other men very angry!

They got even angrier when Uncle and the chief's daughter got married!

Glooskap knew trouble was brewing. "The men will try to get revenge tomorrow," he warned Uncle after the wedding. "But you can escape by jumping over the lodge. You will jump once, then twice, but the third time will be hard for you. Yet this must be."

The next day, Uncle looked up at the tall lodge with its smoking chimney. How could he possibly jump over it?

Yet, when the men approached him, Uncle magically jumped over the lodge. Then he jumped over it again. But the third time...

Uncle got stuck on the poles of the chimney. Ouch! They were hot!

Thanks to Glooskap, Uncle survived. His back became a hard shell with smoky marks. Uncle was now a turtle!

But Uncle was still not safe. "The men will try to get you again," Glooskap warned. "You must convince them to throw you in the lake, because there you will be safe."

So Uncle pretended he was scared of the water and the mean men threw him right in!

And there, Uncle lived a long and happy life as a turtle, safe in his shell!

The next story is set in ancient Greece.

The god Hermes loved to play the harp. But the only animal that enjoyed his sweet music was the slow, shell-less turtle.

One day, as Hermes played, he was stung by a bee. "Ouch!" said Hermes, dropping his harp.

The harp landed right on the turtle's back! Hermes decided to reward his loyal fan. He allowed the turtle to keep the harp as a shell that would protect him forever.

Here is my favorite story. It's the one my parents told me when I was little.

Long ago, when the world was new, the Creator gave each animal something to make it special. Some got sharp teeth or claws. Others got horns, stingers, or fins.

But by the time the slow turtle arrived, the Creator's box of Special Stuff was empty, and he was taking his lunch break!

The turtle sighed. "Now I'll never be special,"
he said to the Creator. "And I'm so slow I probably
won't even survive."

"Of course you'll survive," the Creator said kindly.
Then he put his empty soup bowl on the turtle's
back. "You shall have a shell for protection so you
won't need to be fierce or fast. With this shell you
can be slow and safe forever."

So the soup bowl became the turtle's shell. And he lived slowly and happily ever after.

How do YOU think the turtle got its shell?

We may never know how the turtle really got its shell. But here are some fun facts we do know:

TURTLE TIME

Turtles have been around for over 200 million years. They were on Earth with the first dinosaurs!

Turtles live longer than other vertebrates (animals with spines). The oldest official record is of a turtle that lived in a British zoo for 116 years.

TURTLE TYPES

There are about 220 different kinds of turtles. They fall into three main groups:

Tortoises, which live on land, have heavy, domed shells, thick scaly legs, and toes with claws. They live in warm regions throughout the world.

Marine turtles, which live in the salt water of oceans and seas, have light, flat shells and flippers instead of feet. The flippers help them swim fast.

Freshwater turtles have a leathery covering on their shell. They eat fish, snails, and other animals.

TURTLE BITES

Turtles don't have teeth. Instead, they bite their food with the sharp ridges on their jaws.

Baby turtles have an egg tooth to help them hatch out of their shell. They lose this tooth soon after birth.